~ *Little Women* ~

BULLSEYE CHILLERS™

Little Women

By Louisa May Alcott
Adapted by Monica Kulling

Bullseye Step into Classics™

Random House 🏠 New York

Cover design by Fabia Wargin Design and Creative Media Applications, Inc.

A BULLSEYE BOOK PUBLISHED BY RANDOM HOUSE, INC.
Text copyright © 1994 by Random House, Inc.
Cover illustration copyright © 1994 by Claire Wood
All rights reserved under International and Pan-American Copyright Conventions. Published in the United States by Random House, Inc., New York, and simultaneously in Canada by Random House of Canada Limited, Toronto.

Library of Congress Cataloging-in-Publication Data:
Kulling, Monica. Little women / by Louisa May Alcott ; adapted by Monica Kulling.
  p. cm. — (Bullseye step into classics)
SUMMARY: Chronicles the joys and sorrows of the four March sisters as they grow into young ladies in nineteenth-century New England. ISBN: 0-679-86175-0
[1. Family life—Fiction. 2. Sisters—Fiction. 3. New England—Fiction.]
I. Alcott, Louisa May, 1832–1888. Little women. II. Title. III. Series.
PZ7.K9490155Li 1994 [Fic]—dc20 93-38237

First Random House Bullseye Books edition: 1994

Manufactured in the United States of America   6 7 8 9 10

Contents

Chapter One

A Merry Christmas

The four March sisters sat in the living room. A fire crackled in the fireplace. It was the day before Christmas, but the girls weren't very happy.

"Christmas won't be Christmas without presents," said Jo. She was lying on the rug.

"It's awful to be poor," said Meg, sighing. She was the oldest. She looked at her shabby dress as she spoke.

"And it's not fair!" exclaimed Amy. She was the youngest. "Some girls have lots of pretty things. And other girls have nothing at all."

"We've got Father and Mother and one another," said Beth. Beth was the shy one. She always looked on the bright side of things.

"We haven't got Father," said Jo sadly. "And we might not have him for a very long time."

The girls were suddenly silent. Light from the fire shone on their faces. They were thinking of Father. He was fighting in a war far away. He wouldn't be home for Christmas. And there wouldn't be Christmas presents because there was no money.

"We each have a dollar!" exclaimed Jo. "We could at least buy something for ourselves." Jo loved to read and wanted to buy a new book.

"I'll spend my dollar on music," said Beth.

"I'll spend mine on drawing pencils," said Amy. She was always drawing.

Meg didn't say a word. She wanted so many pretty things that she didn't know where to begin.

Beth put Marmee's slippers in front of the fire to warm them. The girls' mother would soon be home. This thought cheered them up.

"Marmee needs a new pair," said Beth. She looked at her mother's worn slippers.

"I'm the man of the family now that Papa's gone," said Jo. She was the second-oldest and a tomboy. "It's my job to take care of Marmee. I'll buy the slippers."

"I'll tell you what," said Beth. "Let's each get Mother something for Christmas and not get anything for ourselves."

The girls were excited as they planned what to get their mother. After deciding on the presents, they worked on the Christmas night play.

Every Christmas Jo wrote a play. The girls put on the play for family and friends. They were practicing their lines when Marmee walked in.

"Hello, my merry girls," said Mother. Marmee worked as a volunteer for the Soldiers' Aid Society. She had spent the day packing boxes to send to the men. Today she brought happy news: a letter from Father!

"Gather round, girls," said Mrs. March. "Here's a nice, long letter from Father. He is well and sends his Christmas greetings."

Mother read the letter to her eager daughters. It was a cheerful, hopeful letter. In it Father described army life. He described the marches and the men. But he didn't describe the hardships. He didn't want to worry his girls. Father wrote:

Take care of your mother, my loving children. Do your duty faithfully. I know that when I get home I will be fonder and prouder than ever of my little women.

Mother finished the letter. The girls were silent. How they missed Father!

"This time without Father will be hard," said Mother. "It will be like a long journey. And you will be like pilgrims on this journey. You will have to be strong and carry your burdens bravely."

"I wish we had a guidebook to help us on our way," said Jo.

"Look under your pillows Christmas morning," said Mother with a smile.

On Christmas morning Jo was the first to awake. Under her pillow was a little Bible with a red cover. Beth and Amy woke up next, then Meg. Each girl found a Bible under her pillow. Each Bible had a different color cover.

"Let's read a little this morning," said Meg. Meg could be vain and self-centered at times. *This* morning her sweetness shone through. Her sisters happily followed her good example.

The girls went downstairs for breakfast. Marmee was gone. When she returned, she told them about a poor woman she had visited. Mrs. Hummel had six children and a newborn baby. Mrs. Hummel's children were cold and hungry.

"My girls, will you give them your breakfast as a Christmas present?" asked Mother.

The girls were hungry. But it didn't take long for them to agree. They gathered up their breakfast and took it to the neighbor.

"That's loving our neighbor better than ourselves," said Meg when they returned. The girls had bread and milk for breakfast. But it felt good to help a neighbor in need.

After breakfast the girls gave Mother her presents. Marmee was delighted with her new slippers and her new handkerchief. She loved the gloves and the rose sprinkled with perfume.

"You are wonderful girls," she said.

In the afternoon the girls prepared for the play. They built a forest and a cave on their homemade stage. Christmas night a dozen friends watched the curtain rise on "The Witch's Curse."

The audience loved the play. Jo was Roderigo, the hero. He had to rescue Zara, his love, from the evil Hugo. Roderigo climbed a tower to rescue Zara.

The tower rose to the ceiling. It couldn't hold Jo's weight. It fell over with a crash! Jo and Meg, who was playing Zara, were buried under the rubble. But the play continued, through the audience's laughter, to the end.

Then Mother announced a Christmas surprise—a late-night feast! Bouquets of beautiful flowers were in the middle of the table. There were two kinds of ice cream, cake, fruit, and French candies. The sight of this splendid feast took everyone's breath away.

"Is it fairies?" asked Amy.

"Santa Claus must have brought this," said Beth.

"Maybe rich Aunt March had a change of heart," said Jo.

Jo took care of her father's cranky aunt. She found it hard to believe Aunt March could do something this nice.

But the goodies were not from Aunt March. Mr. Laurence, the old gentleman next-door, had sent his grandson over with them.

"I'd love to meet that Laurence boy," said Jo. "He looks as if he could use some fun. Maybe next year we'll invite him to our play!"

So ended the March family's Christmas day. It had been merry, even though Father was never far from their thoughts.

Chapter Two

The Laurence Boy

"Jo! Jo! Where are you?" cried Meg. She was calling up into the attic.

"I'm here!" Jo called down.

Meg climbed the narrow stairs. The attic was Jo's favorite spot in the house. Here she could eat apples and read in peace. A pet rat, Scrabble, lived nearby. Scrabble didn't mind Jo's company a bit. Today Jo was wrapped in a quilt.

"I have news!" exclaimed Meg. "Both of us are invited to Mrs. Gardiner's New Year's Eve party. It's tomorrow night! What should we wear?"

"What's the use in asking that?" said Jo.

"You know we'll have to wear our cotton dresses. We haven't got anything else."

"I wish that I had silk," sighed Meg. "Mother says I have to wait until I'm eighteen to wear silk. Two years seems so long."

"Your dress is as good as new," said Jo. "Mine is a mess. It has a burn and a tear in it."

"You'll have to sit all you can," said Meg. "Keep your back out of sight. Then no one will notice."

Jo frowned at her older sister.

"I will wear a new ribbon in my hair," continued Meg. She loved parties. "Marmee will lend me her little pearl pin. My slippers are lovely. My gloves aren't so clean. But they're better than yours."

"I spilled lemonade on mine," said Jo. "Who needs gloves anyway?" Jo didn't care about clothes.

"You must wear gloves," said Meg.

"Gloves are more important than any-thing else. I won't go if you don't wear gloves."

"Then I'll stay right here," said Jo.

"No, you won't," said Meg. "Can't you make your old gloves do?"

"I know," said Jo. "Why don't we each wear one clean glove of yours and carry one dirty one of mine? Then our gloves will look like new."

"Your hands are bigger than mine," said Meg. "You'll stretch my glove."

"Then I won't wear gloves," said Jo. "I don't care what people say!" She went back to her book.

"You may have my glove, you may!" exclaimed Meg. "Just don't stain it, and do behave nicely. Don't put your hands behind your back and don't swear."

"Don't worry," said Jo. "I'll act like a lady. Now go answer your note. I want to finish this book."

New Year's Eve, Jo and Meg dressed for the party. They looked lovely in their simple dresses. Each wore a clean glove and carried a dirty one.

"Have a good time, dearies!" said Mrs. March. "Don't eat too much, and leave at eleven. I almost forgot. Have you both got pocket-handkerchiefs?"

"Yes," said Jo.

"A real lady always has neat boots, gloves, *and* a handkerchief," said Meg. She loved to dress up and act fancy.

"If I do anything wrong at the party, give me a wink," said Jo.

"Winking isn't ladylike," said Meg. "I'll raise my eyebrows instead."

Mrs. Gardiner met Jo and Meg at the door. Inside there was laughter, music, and happy conversation. Meg knew Sallie, Mrs. Gardiner's oldest daughter, and felt comfortable right away.

Jo was left alone. She stood with her

back to the wall. She tried to hide the burn in her dress. She was uncomfortable. She felt like a pony in a flower garden.

Jo heard a group of boys talking about skating. Jo loved to skate. She wished she could join the boys. But Meg's raised eyebrows stopped her.

A dance was announced. A tall boy with red hair walked toward Jo. He was going to ask Jo to dance. But Jo didn't want to dance. She slipped behind a curtain to hide…and found herself face to face with the Laurence boy.

"I didn't know anyone was here," said Jo. She was about to leave.

But the boy laughed. "Stay if you like," he said.

"Won't I bother you?" asked Jo.

"Not at all," said the boy. "I came back here because I don't know many people. I felt strange."

"Thanks for the Christmas feast," said

Jo. "We had such a good time eating it."

"Grandpa sent it," said the boy.

"But you put the idea in his head. Didn't you?" asked Jo.

The boy smiled. His name was Theodore. He liked to be called Laurie. Jo's name was Josephine, but she liked to be called Jo.

"Do you like parties?" asked Jo.

"Sometimes," said Laurie. "I've lived in Europe for many years. I don't know how they do things over here."

Laurie had gone to school in Switzerland. He had been to Paris and could speak French.

"I love to hear people talk about their travels," said Jo. She asked Laurie questions about school and holidays and walking trips.

Jo liked the Laurence boy. She forgot about her dress. She forgot about Meg's raised eyebrows. She wanted to know how old Laurie was.

"I suppose you are going to college soon?" asked Jo.

"No," said Laurie. "I'm only fifteen. I'll be sixteen next month."

Jo and Laurie talked and talked. Meanwhile, Meg danced and danced. Meg's pretty shoes were too tight. Soon she was limping. She had sprained her ankle.

"I knew those silly shoes would hurt your feet," said Jo. She was rubbing Meg's sore ankle. Laurie had brought Meg a drink and some ice.

"How will we get home?" asked Meg. "A carriage is too expensive."

"Ride with me in my grandfather's carriage," said Laurie. "I always leave parties early. I do!"

The girls rode in the carriage. Laurie sat outside next to the driver, so Meg could keep her foot up.

"I saw you with the redheaded boy," said Jo. "Was he nice?"

"His hair is auburn, not red," said Meg.

"And he is very polite."

"He danced like a grasshopper on fire," said Jo. "Laurie and I couldn't help laughing. Did you hear us?"

"No, but it was very rude," said Meg. "Where were you hiding, anyway?"

Jo told Meg about her adventures. When the carriage stopped in front of the March house, the girls thanked Laurie.

Jo and Meg had enjoyed the party. Old dresses, dirty gloves, and tight shoes couldn't keep them from having a good time.

Chapter Three

The Girls Carry On

"How hard it is to be a pilgrim," said Meg. The week of parties and free time was over. They didn't feel like going back to work.

"I wish it could be Christmas and New Year all the time," said Jo. "Wouldn't it be fun?"

"Oh, yes!" exclaimed Meg. "I love little suppers and going to parties and reading and resting. And not going to work. I'm so fond of luxury."

"Well, we can't have a life of luxury," said Jo. "So stop grumbling. We must carry our loads as cheerfully as Marmee does. Sometimes I find Aunt March hard

to bear. But if I carried her without com-
plaining, she would seem lighter."

The thought made Jo cheerful. But not
Meg. She hated being poor. She remembered when her family had money. Now
she took care of the children of a rich
family. Every day she saw how easy their
life was.

"I will never have any fun," said Meg.
"I will have to moil and toil all my days. I
will only have little bits of fun, now and
then. I will get old and ugly and sour.
And all because I'm poor!"

Everyone was unhappy that morning.
Beth was lying on the sofa with a
headache. She was playing with the cat
and its three kittens. Amy was upset. She
hadn't done her homework, and now she
couldn't find her boots.

"There never was such a crabby family!" cried Jo, spilling a bottle of ink on
the table.

"And you're the crabbiest person in it!" exclaimed Amy.

"Beth, if you don't keep your awful cats down in the cellar I'll have someone drown them," said Meg. One of Beth's kittens had jumped on Meg's back and stuck in its claws.

Mrs. March was writing a letter that had to be mailed that day. She kept making mistakes.

"Girls, girls, do be quiet for one minute!" said Mrs. March. "I have to get this letter off by the early mail. I can't think with all this noise."

Meg and Jo each grabbed a hot breakfast bun. They said good-bye to their mother and their sisters.

"Cuddle your cats, and get over your headache, Bethy," said Jo. "Good-bye, Marmee."

When Mr. March had lost his money, Aunt March had asked to adopt one of the girls. But the family had refused.

"We wouldn't give up one of our girls for a million dollars. Rich or poor, we will stay together. We are happy with one another."

The two older girls were glad to help the family by working. Meg took care of the King children. Jo was Aunt March's companion.

Aunt March was cranky and hard to please. The best part of the job was Aunt March's large library.

Every day Jo read to Aunt March. The old woman always fell asleep. Then Jo would read what she wanted to read until her aunt woke up.

Beth stayed at home and helped keep the house neat. Her shyness made school painful. So Beth used to do her lessons at home with Father. Now that Father was gone, Beth did her lessons on her own.

Beth loved music. The keys on the

family's old piano were yellow with age. Sometimes the notes sounded sour. Beth wanted them to sound sweet. She worked and worked. If only there was money for music lessons. If only the family could afford a better piano.

Twelve-year-old Amy went to school. She had many friends and was able to please without trying. Her love for drawing often got her into trouble. Sometimes the teacher caught her drawing instead of doing her work.

"Has anybody anything to tell?" asked Meg. It was the end of the day. The girls were sewing together. "I'm dying for some amusement."

"I saw something this morning that I forgot to tell at dinner," said Beth.

Everyone stopped sewing to listen.

"Mr. Laurence was in the fish shop this morning," said Beth. "He didn't see me because I was hiding behind a barrel. A poor woman came in with a pail and mop. She asked Mr. Cutter, the fish man, if he would let her do some scrubbing for a bit of fish to feed her children. Mr. Cutter was in a hurry and said, 'No.'

"Then guess what Mr. Laurence did? He hooked up a huge fish with his cane and held it out to the woman. 'Go along and cook it,' he said.

"The woman hurried out of the shop holding the slippery fish in her arms. She looked so happy! Wasn't that good of Mr. Laurence?"

The girls loved Beth's story. Then they asked Mother for a story.

"I was making jackets for the men today," said Mother. "And I started to worry about Father. I worried about what we would do if he didn't come home from the war. Then an old man told me he had four sons in the army. Two are dead, one is in prison, and one is sick in a Washington hospital.

"I said to the old man, 'You've done a great deal for your country.'

"'Not at all,' he said to me. 'I'd go myself if I could. But as I can't, I give my sons freely.'"

Mother looked down at her hands. "The old man was happy to give his all. I was ashamed of myself. I've given only one man. He has given four. His last two sons are miles away. My four girls are at home to comfort me. I felt so rich and happy thinking of my blessings."

The girls were ashamed. They had complained so much that day. Life had seemed so hard. They had forgotten how blessed they were to have one another.

"We need that lesson, Marmee," said Jo. "And we won't forget it."

Chapter Four

Making Friends with Neighbors

"What in the world are you doing, Jo?" asked Meg. It was snowing. Jo was dressed in her boots and coat. She carried a broom in one hand and a shovel in the other.

"Going out for exercise," said Jo. She had a twinkle in her eye.

"I should think that the two long walks you took this morning would be enough exercise," said Meg. "Stay by the fire. It's too cold to go outside."

"I'm not a cat," said Jo. "I don't want to doze all day by the fire. I like adventure, and I'm going to find some."

The snow was light. Jo quickly swept a path around the garden. The garden lay between the Marches' old brown house and the Laurences' stone mansion next-door.

Jo hoped to catch sight of Laurie as she swept. She hadn't spoken with him since the party. She had heard that he was sick.

"There he is," thought Jo. She saw his curly black head in the window. He was leaning on his thin hand, staring into the distance.

Jo threw a soft snowball at the window. Laurie smiled and opened the window.

"How are you feeling?" called Jo.

"Better, thank you," said Laurie. "I've been stuck inside with a cold all week."

"What are you doing for fun?" asked Jo.

"Nothing," said Laurie. "It's as dead as a graveyard around here."

"Don't you read?" asked Jo.

"Grandfather says I'll ruin my eyes if I read when I'm sick," said Laurie. "My teacher, Mr. Brooke, sometimes reads to me. But I can't ask him all the time."

"You need cheering up," said Jo. "I'll be right back!"

She dashed home. She was soon back with a pudding Meg had made and two of Beth's kittens. The kittens made Laurie laugh.

"Forgive me for being rude," said Laurie shyly. "I often watch your family in the evenings. Sometimes you forget to pull the curtains. I see all of you sitting around the table. Your mother's face is so kind. I haven't got a mother, you know."

"Why don't you come over whenever you wish?" asked Jo.

"Grandpa is afraid I might be a bother to strangers," said Laurie.

"We're not strangers," said Jo. 'We're neighbors."

The doctor arrived. Jo went to the library. She walked around the room and stopped in front of a painting.

The old man in the painting was Laurie's grandfather. Jo had never met Mr. Laurence.

"I wouldn't be afraid of him," said Jo, speaking aloud. "He's got kind eyes. He's not as handsome as my own grandfather, but I like him."

"Thank you, ma'am," said a gruff voice behind her. It was Mr. Laurence!

Jo blushed. Her face turned beet red. He had heard every word!

"So you're not afraid of me?" said the old gentleman.

"Not much, sir," said Jo.

"And I'm not as handsome as your grandfather. But you like me just the same?" said the old gentleman.

"Yes, I do, sir," said Jo.

This answer pleased Mr. Laurence. He gave a short laugh and shook hands with Jo. He asked her to stay for tea.

At tea Mr. Laurence saw how well Jo and Laurie got along. Their lively chatter brought life to the boy's face.

"That lad is lonely," thought Mr. Laurence. "It's good for him to have friends his own age." He had liked Jo's grandfather for his brave spirit. They had been friends many years ago. Now he liked Jo for the same reason.

At home Jo told her sisters about her visit. Marmee said Laurie could come over whenever he wanted.

And so the neighbors became friends. The new friendship grew fast, like grass in the spring. Shy Beth was the only one who found it hard to visit. Mr. Laurence could be loud and gruff.

Mr. Laurence found out that Beth was afraid of him. He also found out that she liked music. He went over to talk to Mrs. March.

"My grandson doesn't play the piano as much as he used to," said Mr. Laurence. "Do your girls like music?"

Beth listened quietly. She didn't say a word. How she longed to play the Laurences' grand piano!

"If one of your girls would like to play my piano," said Mr. Laurence, "all she has to do is come over. She won't have to talk to anyone. She won't even have to see anyone. She can shut the door and play as much as she likes. And she won't disturb a soul."

Marmee smiled. She knew Mr. Laurence was thinking of Beth. Beth left her corner and came over.

"Do you like music?" asked Mr. Laurence.

"Yes, sir," said Beth. "I would love to play your grand piano."

From that day on, Beth spent her after-
noons playing the Laurence piano. There
was always new sheet music waiting for
her. She never knew that Mr. Laurence
often opened his study door to listen to
her play.

Beth wanted to thank Mr. Laurence.
But how? She carefully sewed him a pair
of slippers and wrote a short note. Laurie
slipped the package on the old man's
study table.

A few days later, Beth came home to a
wonderful surprise: a beautiful little
upright piano! And a letter to her from
Mr. Laurence.

The piano had belonged to Mr. Laurence's granddaughter. She had died long
ago. Mr. Laurence gave the piano to Beth
because she reminded him of his granddaughter.

Beth's face glowed with delight when
she played her new piano.

"I'll go over right now and thank him!" she exclaimed.

"That's a surprise," said Meg. "Beth going next-door like that."

Beth knocked on the study door. Her knees trembled a little. A gruff voice called out, "Come in!"

Beth entered the room and walked right up to Mr. Laurence.

"I came to thank you, sir, for—" But Beth didn't finish.

Mr. Laurence looked so friendly. Beth forgot what she wanted to say. She just put her arms around Mr. Laurence's neck and kissed him.

If the roof of the house had blown away at that moment, it would not have been as big a surprise. Old Mr. Laurence had made a friend in Beth. And Beth was never afraid of her neighbor again.

Chapter Five

Amy's Rough Road

Amy had a pickled lime problem.

"Everyone is sucking limes in school these days," she told Meg. "My friends are always treating. I can't because I never have any money.

"I owe at least a dozen pickled limes. If I don't buy some limes soon, my friends will think I'm cheap."

So Meg gave Amy a quarter to buy pickled limes.

The next day Amy brought twenty-four delicious pickled limes to class. She hid the bag inside her desk.

Jenny Snow knew Amy was not going to give her a lime. She told the teacher that Amy was hiding a bag of limes.

The word *limes* was like fire to gunpowder for the teacher, Mr. Davis. He was trying to stop the girls from eating the awful things in class.

"Miss March, bring your limes to my desk, if you please!" ordered Mr. Davis.

Amy was surprised. She hadn't seen Jenny tell Mr. Davis. Shaking out half a dozen to keep, she brought the rest to Mr. Davis.

"Is that all?" asked Mr. Davis. He looked inside the bag.

"Not quite," said Amy. She couldn't tell a lie. She went to get the rest.

"Now take those disgusting things and throw them out the window," said Mr. Davis. "Two at a time."

This was too much for the girls. All those plump, juicy limes smashing to the ground! One lime lover burst into tears at the sight of the limes sailing out the window.

"Miss March, you have broken my rule," said Mr. Davis. "Hold out your hand."

Jenny Snow gave a satisfied hiss.

Amy braced herself for the sting of the ruler. She took the blows bravely. They were few and not that hard. Amy was Mr. Davis's favorite pupil.

Amy had never been hit before. She felt ashamed. But there was more.

Mr. Davis made Amy stand in front of the class. Amy stood without moving. She stared at a sea of faces for fifteen long minutes. Her face was white from the pain in her heart.

At recess Amy ran home crying. She needed the warmth of her family. Meg washed her sister's hand with cream. Beth looked on sadly. And Jo was so angry she wanted to have Mr. Davis arrested on the spot.

Mother was upset that Amy had broken one of the teacher's rules. But she was more upset that Mr. Davis had hit her daughter.

"You can have a vacation from school, Amy," said Marmee. "But I want you to study a little every day with Beth.

"You have many talents, Amy," continued Mother. "But I have noticed that you are getting too proud. The teacher was wrong to correct you the way he did. But please remember, talent is most charming when the owner is humble."

Before school ended that day, Jo took a letter from her mother to Mr. Davis. Jo's eyes were icy as she handed the letter to Mr. Davis. Then Jo emptied Amy's desk and left the room.

The following day was Saturday. In the afternoon Amy smelled a secret. Jo and Meg were on their way out of the house.

"Where are you going?" she asked.

"Little girls shouldn't ask questions," said Jo sharply.

"You're going to the hall to see that

new play, aren't you?" asked Amy. "Laurie is going with you, isn't he?"

"Maybe Mother wouldn't mind if Amy came with us," said Meg.

"If she goes, I don't," said Jo. "Laurie will give her his seat. Then he'll have to sit alone."

"You'll be sorry for this, Jo March," warned Amy.

And Jo *was* sorry. The next day she couldn't find her little book.

Jo had been writing stories for several years. She had spent months copying them into a new book. Now her book was lost. Jo thought of Amy at once.

"Where is my book, Amy?" asked Jo.

"I don't know," said Amy.

"That's a fib!" exclaimed Jo in a fury. "You hid it!"

"I didn't," said Amy. "I burned it up. You'll never see it again!"

"You wicked, wicked girl!" exclaimed

Jo. "I can never write those stories again. I'll never forgive you as long as I live!"

Jo shook Amy and rushed out of the room crying.

Amy was sorry for what she had done. The whole family loved Jo's stories. They couldn't believe that Amy would do such a thing.

Amy said she was sorry. But Jo refused to forgive her.

The next day Jo wouldn't speak to Amy. Amy tried again and again to get Jo to forgive her. But Jo wouldn't say a word. She ignored Amy.

In the afternoon Jo went out to skate with Laurie. Meg told Amy to try to catch Jo while she was in a good mood. So Amy rushed to the edge of the river. She put on her skates.

Jo saw her from the corner of her eye. But she wouldn't look Amy's way. The longer Jo stayed mad at her sister, the easier it got to ignore her.

Winter was almost over. The ice on the river was soft in the middle. Jo and Laurie knew that they must keep close to the shore. Amy didn't know. She skated to the middle of the river.

Suddenly the ice cracked. Amy fell through the ice with a loud cry. Jo's heart stood still.

Jo and Laurie raced to rescue Amy. Amy was shivering, dripping, and crying when they got her home. Mother wrapped Amy in a warm blanket in front of the fire. Soon she was asleep.

"Are you sure she is safe?" asked Jo. Her hands were cut from the ice. Marmee was bandaging them.

"Quite safe, dear," said Marmee. She could see how upset Jo was. "She isn't hurt. She won't even catch a cold. You brought her home so quickly."

"Thanks to Laurie. Not me," sobbed Jo.

"She might have died. I was so mad. Mother, sometimes my anger scares me."

"Don't cry so much, my dear," said Marmee. "You think your temper is the worst in the world. But mine used to be just like it."

"Yours, Mother?" asked Jo. "But you never get angry!"

"I've learned not to show my anger. That's all," said Marmee. "I leave the room when I'm mad. I bite my tongue before I say the angry words that come so easily."

How comforting to know that Mother also had to control her temper! Jo promised to try harder.

Before going to bed, Jo leaned over her sleeping sister. Amy woke. She opened her eyes and held out her arms to Jo. The girls hugged each other close. All was forgiven in that one embrace.

Chapter Six

Meg Lives the Good Life

It was a morning in April. And Meg could hardly believe her good luck. Since the King children had measles, Meg wasn't working. She was free to visit her friend Ann Moffat for two weeks. Her sisters were helping her pack.

"Imagine two whole weeks of fun," said Jo. She was folding Meg's skirts.

"And the weather is so lovely," said Beth. She was sorting neck and hair ribbons.

"I wish I was going to have a fine time," said Amy. "And wear all these nice things."

"I'll tell you all about it when I get back," promised Meg.

"What did Marmee give you out of the treasure box?" asked Amy. Mrs. March had saved "treasures" for the girls from when the family had money. The girls would get them at the proper time.

"A pair of silk stockings. A pretty carved fan. And a lovely blue sash," said Meg. "I wanted the silk dress. But there isn't time to make it over. My cotton party dress will have to do."

"You look like an angel in that dress," said Amy.

There would be several parties at the Moffats'. Meg wanted to look as if she belonged.

"My bonnet doesn't look like Annie's," said Meg. "And Mother bought me a green umbrella. I wanted black."

"Change it," said Jo.

"That might hurt Marmee's feelings,"

said Meg. "It seems the more one gets, the more one wants, doesn't it?"

Meg arrived at the Moffats' in good spirits. The Moffats were rich but kind. Their house was elegant. Their meals were grand. The Moffat girls, Belle and Annie, had everything they wanted.

Meg liked riding in a fine carriage and going to plays and the opera. She loved having nothing to do but enjoy herself. The more she saw of the Moffat girls' pretty things, the more Meg longed to be rich.

One evening there was a small party. Meg's best cotton dress looked old and shabby. The Moffat girls were wearing silk. But they weren't unkind.

Annie helped Meg tie her sash. Belle fixed her hair. Meg thought they felt sorry for her because she was poor. A hurt, heavy feeling began to grow inside her.

Flowers arrived from Laurie just before the party. And there was a note from Mother. Meg's heart was light once more. She quickly made up little bouquets for her friends. Her old dress seemed fine with a rose on it.

Meg enjoyed the party. She was praised for looking so lovely. Annie made Meg sing. And someone said Meg had a very fine voice.

Meg's fun ended when she overheard Mrs. Moffat talking to a friend.

"I think the boy is sixteen or seventeen," said Mrs. Moffat.

"It would be wonderful if one of those girls were to marry that rich young man," said the friend.

"I'm sure Mrs. March has her plans," said Mrs. Moffat. "If she's smart, she'll play her cards right."

They were talking about Laurie! How could they? Meg was ready to cry and rush home. Since that was impossible, Meg tried to seem happy.

Meg didn't sleep much that night. She woke up tired. There was another party that evening. Laurie was invited because the Moffats thought he was Meg's boyfriend.

That evening Meg put on the same dress she wore the evening before.

"Why don't you send home for another dress?" asked Annie's friend Sallie. Annie and Belle glared at her.

"I don't have any other," admitted Meg. How hard that was to say!

"I've a lovely blue silk that's too small for me," said Belle. "Do please me by wearing it."

Meg couldn't refuse such a kind offer.

Annie and Belle curled Meg's hair. They polished her neck and arms with scented powder. But Meg didn't let them put rouge on her lips.

Then they laced Meg into a sky blue dress. It was so tight Meg could hardly breathe.

Next came bracelets, a necklace, a brooch, and even earrings. And at last— Meg's dream—blue silk boots with high heels. A bouquet in a silver holder finished her off.

"Come, see yourself," said Annie.

Meg looked in the mirror. She *was* beautiful!

Then the Moffat girls showed Meg how to walk in heels while carrying her long skirts.

Meg felt strange. But she made an elegant entrance. She acted the part of a fine lady as if it were made for her.

She was playing with her fan and laughing at a young gentleman's weak jokes when she saw Laurie. She rushed over to shake his hand.

"The girls dressed me up for fun," said

Meg. She saw how Laurie looked at her. "Do you like me this way?"

"I don't like it. You look so grown-up. Not like yourself at all," said Laurie. "Too much fuss and feathers."

"Why, you're the rudest boy I ever saw!" said Meg. She walked away.

Laurie didn't see her again until supper.

Meg was drinking wine and flirting with two young men. "That stuff will give you a bad headache," whispered Laurie. "You know your mother doesn't like it."

"Tomorrow I'll be myself again," said Meg. "Tonight I'm a doll that does silly things."

The next day was Sunday. Meg went home.

"Home is a nice place, even though it isn't splendid," said Meg. She was sitting with Jo and Marmee that evening.

"I'm glad to hear you say so, dear," said Marmee. "I was afraid home would seem

dull to you after your time with the Moffats."

Meg told her mother and Jo how silly
she had been at the party.

"Everyone said I was a beauty. I
romped and drank wine and tried to flirt.
I knew I was acting silly, but I felt so flat-
tered."

Then she told them about the gossip
she had overheard.

"If that isn't the silliest rubbish I ever
heard!" exclaimed Jo.

"I hate to have people think such
things about us and Laurie," said Meg.

"Never repeat that foolish gossip," said
Mrs. March. "And forget it as soon as you
can.

"I *do* have plans for my daughters,"
continued Mrs. March. "I want each of
you to be admired, loved, and respected.
And I want you to marry wisely. Not for
money, but for love. All the riches in the

world can't make a person happy. Will you remember this?"

"We will, Marmee, we will!" cried both girls with all their hearts.

Chapter Seven

The Lazy Days
of Summer

It was the first of June. Meg and Jo were starting their summer holidays. Laurie surprised them with a post office made out of an old birdhouse.

"You can put letters, stories, books, and parcels in the post office," Laurie told the girls. "I'm giving you each a key. Beth can be the postmistress, since she's home the most."

The girls started to use the post office right away. They mailed things to one another and to the Laurences.

Laurie mailed flowers to Mrs. March every morning. Mother often mailed little notes to her daughters.

"Here are your flowers, Mother," said Beth one morning. She was delivering the mail. "Laurie never forgets them. And here's a letter and a glove for Miss Meg March."

"I left my gloves at the Laurences'," said Meg. "Where's the other one? Did you drop it in the garden?"

"No, I'm sure I didn't," said Beth. "There was only one in the post office."

"My letter is just the English words to a German song," said Meg. "I think Laurie's teacher, Mr. Brooke, wrote it. The writing isn't Laurie's."

Mother looked at Meg and smiled.

Meg looked so grown-up, sitting in her corner and sewing.

"Two letters for Jo," said Beth.

One letter was from Marmee.

I see your efforts to control your temper. Go

*on, dear, patiently and bravely. Always remember,
no one understands how hard it is as much as
your loving,*

Mother

Jo thanked her mother with a kiss.

Jo's other letter was from Laurie. He
was inviting the March girls on a boating
trip to Longmeadow with his guests from
England. He was bringing everything:
lunch, a tent, croquet—how exciting!

On the day of the picnic the sun
shone brilliantly. A carriage rolled up to
the Laurence mansion.

Laurie's guests had arrived. Kate was
older than Meg. The twins, Fred and
Frank, were Laurie's age. And the youngest, Grace, was nine.

It was not far to Longmeadow. Mr.
Brooke and Fred rowed one boat. Jo and
Laurie rowed the other.

When they reached Longmeadow, the

tent had been set up. Wickets were in place for a game of croquet.

"Let's play!" said Laurie. And the game began.

Jo and Fred almost got into a fight. Jo saw Fred push a ball through a wicket with his toe.

"You pushed it," said Jo. "I saw you. We don't cheat in America."

"I swear it rolled on its own," said Fred. Then he knocked Jo's ball into the bushes.

Jo started to answer, but stopped herself. She didn't want to lose her temper.

It took a few strokes for Jo to catch up with everybody. Fred had almost made her lose the game. But in the end Jo won with a clever stroke.

"Good for you, Jo!" whispered Laurie. "Fred *did* cheat. I saw him. He won't do it again, take my word for it."

After lunch, everyone did whatever

they wished. Kate and Amy sat under a tree to draw. Jo, Laurie, and some of the others played a game. And Mr. Brooke helped Meg with her German.

Meg was reading out loud. "You have a nice accent!" exclaimed Mr. Brooke.

Mr. Brooke looked as if he enjoyed teaching. He *did* like to teach, but he also liked Meg.

"I wish I liked teaching as you do," said Meg.

"You would if you had Laurie for a pupil," said Mr. Brooke. "But soon he will go to college. Then I'll join the army. I have no family and few friends to care if I live or die," he added bitterly.

"Laurie and his grandfather would care a great deal. We would all be very sorry if anything happened to you," said Meg.

"Thank you," said Mr. Brooke. "That means a great deal to me."

After supper there was another game of croquet. At sunset everything was packed up. The whole party floated home down the river. They were singing at the top of their voices.

Chapter Eight

Castles in the Air

Each of the March girls had a dream she hoped would come true someday. They called their dreams "castles in the air."

"Wouldn't it be fun if all our castles in the air could come true?" asked Jo. "And we could live in them?"

Laurie agreed. He also had a castle in the air. He wanted to travel the world and become a famous musician.

Meg dreamed about a life of luxury. She loved fine food, pretty clothes, and beautiful furniture. Jo knew that Meg also wanted a husband and children.

Beth wanted only to continue to live

with her family. As long as she had her piano, and her family was well, Beth was happy.

Amy wanted "to live in Rome and to paint fine pictures and to be the best artist in the whole world."

Jo's castle in the air was as splendid as everyone else's. She wanted a stable of Arabian horses. She wanted rooms and rooms of books. And she wanted a magic inkstand. She wanted her writing to be as famous as Laurie's music.

Jo had the key to her castle. She wrote every day. But she didn't know if all her secret writing would unlock her castle door.

A few days later, Jo was writing in the attic. She scribbled away until the last page was finished. Then she read the story aloud. Scrabble, the rat, paused as if to listen.

"There, I've done my best!" exclaimed

Jo. She tied the pages with a red ribbon. Climbing out a back window, she took a roundabout way to the road. Then she caught the bus into the city.

Jo knew where she was going. The newspaper office was at the top of the stairs, right next-door to the dentist's office.

Laurie was waiting for Jo. He had been at his fencing lesson across the street when he spotted her. He thought Jo had gone to the dentist.

"How many did you have out?" he asked.

"There are two which I want to have come out," said Jo. "But I must wait a week." Jo's eyes twinkled.

"You have a secret, don't you?" said Laurie. "Well, so do I. If you tell me your secret, I'll tell you mine."

"You won't tell anyone at home, will you?" asked Jo.

"Not a word," said Laurie.

"And you won't tease me in private?" asked Jo.

"I never tease," said Laurie.

Jo laughed. Laurie loved to tease.

"Well, I've left two stories with the newspaper," said Jo. "Next week I'll find out if they'll print them."

"Hurray for Miss March the celebrated American author!" Laurie threw his hat into the air and caught it. "What fun to see your stories in print," he added. "They're better than half the rubbish that is published."

Jo's eyes sparkled. It was great to have a friend believe in her.

"What's *your* secret?" asked Jo.

"I may get into trouble for telling you this," said Laurie. "But I know where Meg's lost glove is."

Meg's glove was still missing It hadn't been in the post office. And it wasn't anywhere in the house.

"Is that all?" asked Jo. "That's not much of a secret."

"It is when I tell you where. It's in Mr. Brooke's pocket. He's been carrying it in his pocket for months. Isn't that romantic?" asked Laurie.

"It's disgusting!" said Jo. "I wish you hadn't told me."

"I thought you'd be pleased," said Laurie.

"How could I like someone taking away my Meg?" asked Jo. "No, thank you!"

"You'll be happier when someone comes to take you away," said Laurie.

"I'd like to see anyone try," said Jo.

"So would I!" laughed Laurie. "Race with me down this hill, and you'll feel better."

The two friends raced like wild horses. Jo's hat flew off. Her hairpins scattered behind her.

Jo stopped at the bottom of the hill.

Her cheeks were red. Her hair was a mess. Just then Meg came along, dressed for company. She had been visiting Sallie Gardiner.

"What in the world are you doing here?" Meg asked Jo.

"Collecting leaves," said Jo. She quickly picked up a handful.

"And hairpins," said Laurie. He had a handful of Jo's scattered hairpins.

"You've been running again, haven't you, Jo?" said Meg. "When *will* you stop romping like a boy?"

"Not until I'm stiff and old and have to use a cane," said Jo. "Don't try to make me grow up before my time, Meg. It's hard enough to have you change so suddenly. Let me be a young girl as long as I can."

"Where have you been?" asked Laurie.

"At the Gardiners'," said Meg. "Sallie's been telling me all about Belle Moffat's wedding. It was splendid. And they have gone to spend the winter in Paris. How delightful that must be! I do envy Belle."

"If you care so much about riches, you won't want to marry a poor man," said Jo. This thought pleased her, since she knew Mr. Brooke was poor.

The next two weeks Jo acted strangely. She rushed to the door when the postman rang. She was rude to Mr. Brooke whenever they met. She would stare at Meg sadly. Then she would jump up, run over, and kiss her.

One morning Jo came in with the newspaper. She threw herself on the sofa and pretended to read.

"Anything interesting?" asked Meg.

"Nothing but a story," said Jo. "It doesn't amount to much, I guess."

"Read it to us!" begged Amy.

"Who wrote it?" Beth asked when Jo finished.

"Your sister," Jo said, with a smile.

"You?" cried Meg, dropping her sewing.

How excited everyone was! Beth skipped and sang for joy. Amy had ideas for Jo's next story. And Mrs. March beamed with pride.

"Maybe someday I will be able to earn my living as a writer!" said Jo.

That was Jo's dearest wish, to earn her living as a writer—and to help the girls.

This published story seemed like the first step toward Jo's dream.

Chapter Nine

Mother Goes to Washington

"November is an unpleasant month," said Meg. She stared bleakly out the window.

"That's the reason I was born in it," said Jo.

"Something pleasant should happen now," said Beth. "Then we would think November a delightful month." Beth was always hopeful.

"Two pleasant things are about to happen," said Amy. She was looking out the window too. "Marmee is coming down the street. And Laurie is tramping through the garden. I'm sure he's got something nice to tell us."

They entered together. Mrs. March asked her usual afternoon question.

"Any letter from Father, girls?"

So far there was no letter.

"It's not like Father," said Marmee. "He's as regular as the sun."

Laurie invited the girls for a ride. He agreed to stop at the post office.

The doorbell stopped the planning. It was a telegram.

Mrs. March:
> *Your husband is very sick. Come at once.*
> *Soldiers' Hospital, Washington*

The room grew silent. Suddenly the day seemed bleaker. Everything had changed in one moment.

"I shall go at once," said Marmee. "Help me be strong." The girls gathered around their mother. They hugged her and wept.

Then Mother got busy. The next train for Washington left in the morning. She sent Laurie to Aunt March's with a note. Money was needed for the trip.

Mr. Laurence brought over food, wine, and blankets. Supplies at the army hospital were not always good. Shortly after Mr. Laurence left, Mr. Brooke arrived. He offered to go to Washington with Mrs. March.

Laurie came back with money and a note from Aunt March. She wrote how absurd it was that Mr. March was in the army. She always knew it would come to this.

Mother threw the note into the fire. She put the money in her purse. Her lips were tight as she packed.

Jo had left the house. If she had been in the room, she would have seen Marmee's tight lips. She would have understood that Marmee was trying to control her anger.

Jo returned. She handed her mother twenty-five dollars.

"I didn't steal this money," said Jo. She saw how her mother looked at her.

"I came by it honestly."

Jo took off her bonnet. Her hair was cut short.

"Your hair! Your beautiful hair!" exclaimed Marmee. "My dear girl, there was no need of this."

"The barber paid me for it," said Jo. "It will grow back soon. It will do my brains good to get some air."

"What made you do it?" asked Amy.

Amy thought she would rather have her head cut off than her hair.

"I was wild to do something for Father," said Jo. "I hate to borrow as much as Mother does. And I knew Aunt March would complain, as always.

"I saw long tails of hair in a barber's window yesterday. Today I asked the barber if he would buy *my* hair. He didn't want to at first, because my hair color isn't in demand. When I told him why I wanted to sell my hair, he changed his mind. And here I am! I have saved one lock for you, Marmee."

Mother took the wavy chestnut lock. She laid it in a drawer next to a lock of Father's hair. Sadness like a shadow stole across Mother's face.

Early next morning, Mother and Mr. Brooke left for Washington. There was much hugging and kissing and many promises to write.

The girls kept busy as Marmee had asked them to do. Meg went back to taking care of the King children. Jo went back to Aunt March. And Beth and Amy kept the house in order.

Soon there was news. Mother had arrived. She had already done Father a world of good. He was on the mend. The girls were greatly comforted by this news. Meg wrote:

My Dearest Mother—

Your last letter made us very happy. Mr. Brooke is very kind. He writes often to tell us about Father.

The girls are as good as gold. Jo helps me with sewing and does the hard chores. I'm afraid that she might overdo it, but then I remember that Jo's busyness never lasts long.

Beth is as regular as clockwork. Amy minds me nicely. She does her own hair. And I am teaching her how to mend her stockings.

Mr. Laurence is wonderful. He watches over us like an old mother hen. Laurie and Jo keep us all merry.

We long to have you back. Give our love to Father. I am ever your own,

Meg

Jo sent her mother a freshly written

poem. Beth sent her love and a few pressed flowers. Amy's sweet letter was full of spelling mistakes. She was learning French and tried to use every French word she knew.

Mr. Laurence wrote to tell Mrs. March that the girls were well. Laurie wrote to make her smile. Everyone was waiting, with silent prayers, for Mother and Father to come back.

Chapter Ten

Dark Days

The March girls tried very hard to keep busy. But little by little they grew lazy. Beth was the only one who remained faithful. She even continued to visit poor Mrs. Hummel and her children.

One morning Beth didn't feel well.

"Meg, I wish you'd go and see the Hummels," said Beth. "You know Mother told us not to forget them."

"I'm too tired today," said Meg. She was comfortable in her rocker.

"Will you go, Jo?" asked Beth.

"Too stormy for me," said Jo. She kept forgetting to wear a hat over her short hair. Now she had a cold.

"I thought your cold was better," said Beth.

"Well, it's better for visiting Laurie," said Jo, with a smile. "But not for visiting Mrs. Hummel."

Jo knew this sounded awful. But she was having such a good time resting and reading.

"Why don't you go?" asked Meg.

"I *have* been," said Beth. "Every day. But the baby is sick, and I don't know what to do. Mrs. Hummel goes to work every day, and the baby gets sicker."

Since no one else would go, Beth did. She came home late. She was tired and had a headache. Jo found her in the bathroom, crying.

"What's the matter?" she asked.

"You've had scarlet fever, haven't you?" asked Beth.

"Years ago, when Meg did," said Jo. "Why?"

"Mrs. Hummel's baby died in my lap

this evening," said Beth. "It died before its mother came home. It had scarlet fever."

"My poor dear," said Jo. "How terrible for you! I should have gone." She took her sister in her arms and held her close.

"Oh, Beth," said Jo. "If you get sick, I will never forgive myself!"

Next day Beth had a fever. She waited in bed for the doctor.

Meg wanted to tell Mother that Beth was sick. But Jo thought it was nothing more than a cold.

"Mother can't leave Father, and it will only worry her," said Jo.

Dr. Banks told the girls not to worry. Beth had only a mild case of scarlet fever, and Amy was sent to stay with Aunt March because she'd never had it.

Jo stayed at home and cared for her dearest sister with all the love in her heart.

But each passing day proved the doctor wrong. It wasn't a mild case.

Beth got sicker and sicker. She lay in bed, pale and near death. She didn't know where she was. And she didn't even know her sisters.

A letter from Washington added to the girls' sorrow. Mr. March was worse. He wouldn't be coming home for a long time.

How dark the days were then! How sad and lonely the house was. And how heavy were the hearts of the sisters as they waited.

Then it was that Meg knew what riches were truly worth having—love, protection, peace, and health. These were the *real* blessings of life.

Jo thought of how much Beth's unselfish ways made their family home a happy place.

Amy, at Aunt March's, longed to be home. She remembered how often Beth had done *her* chores. No amount of work would be too much. If only Beth would get better.

The Laurences were worried too. Laurie wandered the March home like a ghost. Mr. Laurence locked the grand piano. He could not bear to be reminded of the young neighbor who used to play it.

Everyone missed Beth. The neighbors sent all sorts of comforts and good wishes, even poor Mrs. Hummel. Those who knew her best were surprised. Shy little Beth had made many friends.

Dr. Banks came twice a day to see Beth. Meg kept a telegram in her desk. She was going to send it should her sister take a turn for the worse.

It was Jo who never left Beth's side. For Beth was Jo's favorite. And Jo couldn't imagine life without Beth.

On December first there was a bitter wind. Snow was falling. When Dr. Banks looked at Beth, he shook his head.

"If Mrs. March can leave her husband, she'd better be sent for," he said.

Jo snatched up the telegram. She rushed out in the storm to mail it. As soon as she returned, Laurie came in. He had a letter from Mrs. March saying that Father was on the mend again. At last, some good news!

"I've sent for Mother," said Jo. "Beth isn't getting better."

The tears began to run down her cheeks. She stretched out her hand to Laurie. The boy took Jo's hand in his.

"Keep hoping for the best," he said. "That will help you, Jo. Soon your mother will be here, and then everything will be right."

"Beth is my dearest sister," said Jo. "I can't give her up. I can't! I can't."

"I don't think she will die," said Laurie. "She's so good, and we all love her so much. I don't believe God will take her away so soon."

"The good and dear people always die," said Jo, sobbing. But slowly her crying quieted. Laurie's words had comforted her. His next words lifted her heart.

"I sent for your mother yesterday," admitted Laurie. "Grandfather thought that we shouldn't wait any longer. Your mother will be here tonight."

"Oh, Laurie! Oh, Mother!" exclaimed Jo. "I'm so glad."

A breath of fresh air seemed to blow through the house. Something better than sunshine made the quiet rooms bright. Even Beth's bird began to chirp. Meg and Jo smiled and hugged each other.

Everyone rejoiced but Beth. She lay near death. The doctor said a change, for better or for worse, would come very soon.

It was past two in the morning. The

house was quiet. Outside, the wind wailed. The snow fell.

Mother wasn't home yet. Jo stood at her bedroom window, waiting. How sad the world looked. Suddenly a cold fear passed through her. "What if Beth is dead, and Meg is afraid to tell me?"

Jo ran to Beth's room. She had to see for herself. To her excited eyes, there was a change. Beth was resting peacefully. Her fever was gone. Color was coming back into her cheeks.

Jo leaned over to kiss Beth's damp brow. Beth opened her eyes and looked at Jo. She smiled weakly, then closed her eyes. She fell into a sound sleep.

"Oh, my goodness me!" exclaimed Jo "The fever's turned."

Meg came over to see for herself. She had been awake for days. Her eyes were heavy. But looking at her beloved sister, Meg's heart was light. Beth was all right. The waiting was over.

It was almost dawn. The sun was rising in all its splendor. The world never looked so lovely.

The sound of bells came from below. Meg and Jo heard Laurie calling from downstairs, "Girls, she's come! She's come!"

Meg and Jo ran downstairs to greet their mother.

Chapter Eleven

Secrets

One evening, while Meg was writing to Father, Jo went upstairs to Beth's room. Beth was getting stronger each day. Still, Marmee never left her side.

"I want to talk to you about Meg," said Jo.

"Beth is asleep," said Mother. "Speak low and tell me all about it."

"Last summer Meg left a pair of gloves over at the Laurences'," said Jo. "Only one was returned. We all forgot about it. Then Laurie told me that Mr. Brooke has the missing glove. He's kept it in his vest pocket all this time," Jo added. "Once it fell out, and Laurie joked about it. Then Mr. Brooke told Laurie that he liked Meg. He didn't dare tell her so because she's so young and he's so poor. Isn't that disgusting?"

"Do you think Meg cares for him?" asked Mother.

"I don't know anything about love and such nonsense!" exclaimed Jo. "Meg doesn't act the way the girls in books do when they're in love. She eats and drinks and sleeps as always. And she only blushes a little when Laurie teases her about Mr. Brooke."

"So you think Meg isn't interested in John?" asked Mother.

"Who?" said Jo. Her mouth fell open.

"Mr. Brooke," said Mother. "Father and I call him John. He took such good care of Father. We think he is an excellent man. We're very fond of him. He's been open to us about Meg. He means to make her a home before he asks her to marry him. I am a little sorry this is happening now. Meg is too young to marry. But we have told him he will have to wait a few years."

"I wish I could marry Meg and keep her safe in the family!" cried Jo.

Jo was upset, but she promised to keep the news to herself.

It didn't take long for Laurie to get the secret out of Jo. He was a little angry that Mr. Brooke hadn't told him first. He decided to play a trick on Mr. Brooke.

The next day Jo was handing out the mail from the post office.

"Here's a note for you, Meg," said Jo. "It's all sealed up! How odd."

Meg cried out as she read it.

"Dear, what is it?" asked Mother.

"Oh, Jo, how could you be so cruel?" Meg hid her face in her hands and cried as if her heart were broken.

"Me! I've done nothing!" exclaimed Jo. "What are you talking about?"

"You wrote this note, and that bad boy helped you. How could you?" sobbed Meg.

Jo and Marmee read the note.

My Dearest Margaret—

Do you love me as I love you? If you do, please give me word before I return. I want to ask your parents for your hand. Mr. Laurence will help me find a good job. And then, my sweet girl, we will be together forever. Send me one word of hope through Laurie,

Your loving John

"So *that's* Laurie's way of paying me back for not keeping my word to Mother," cried Jo. "I'll give him a piece of my mind. Then I'll send him over to apologize!" Jo was at the door.

But Marmee stopped her. "You've

played so many tricks yourself Jo. I want to make sure you didn't have anything to do with this one."

"On my word, Mother, I didn't," said Jo. "I've never seen the note before!"

Marmee saw that Jo was telling the truth.

"If this was my trick, I would have done it better," added Jo. "Besides, Mr. Brooke wouldn't write stuff like this."

"But it looks like his writing," said Meg. She was comparing the note with another one in her hand.

"Oh, Meg, you didn't answer him, did you?" asked Mrs. March. "It's worse than I thought."

"Laurie gave me the first letter a few days ago," began Meg. "He looked as if he didn't know anything about it. I kept the letter a secret. I was deciding what to write back. The way girls in books do. Now I feel so silly! I'll never be able to look Mr. Brooke in the eye again."

"What did you write, dear?" asked Marmee.

"I said I was too young to marry," replied Meg. "I said I didn't wish to have secrets from you. That he should speak with Father. And I said I would be his friend, but nothing more, for a long while."

Jo clapped her hands and laughed. "Wonderful! You're like a lady in a love story! What did he say to that?"

"He wrote that he had never written me a love letter," said Meg. "That he was sorry my sister Jo should play such a mean trick on both of us. Oh, Marmee, I feel so awful!"

Meg leaned against Marmee. Jo tramped around the room calling Laurie names.

"Mr. Brooke didn't send you these letters," said Jo, carefully looking them over.

"Laurie did! He wanted to get back at me because I tried not to share my secret with him. And he kept your letter so he could crow over me with it. He's made trouble for me *and* for you. I mean to make him apologize!"

Jo ran next-door. She didn't tell Laurie why Mother wanted to see him. But when Laurie entered the room and saw Marmee's face, he knew.

Marmee spoke with Laurie alone. When Meg and Jo were called in, they could see he regretted his prank.

"I'll never tell Brooke about this," said Laurie. "I promise. You will forgive me, won't you?"

"It was an unkind thing to do," said Meg. "I didn't think you could be so sly." But then Meg forgave him.

Only Jo wouldn't look at him. She didn't say a word, so Laurie left.

As soon as he was gone, Jo wished she

had said something. She ran next-door. Laurie was locked in his room.

"Grandfather shook me," said Laurie. "Because I wouldn't tell him why your mother wanted me. I would have told him my part in it. But I couldn't without giving Meg away."

"He didn't know we had forgiven you," said Jo.

"He should believe me," replied Laurie. "Instead, he treats me like a baby. I've a mind to run away!"

"If I get Grandpa to apologize for the shaking, will you give up running away?" asked Jo.

"Yes, but you won't be able to do it," said Laurie.

Mr. Laurence was in his library.

"I know that boy's been up to something," he said when Jo entered. "But he won't tell me what it is. And I don't want you protecting him."

"Laurie did do wrong," replied Jo. "But we forgave him and promised not to speak of it again."

"Well, if the boy wasn't talking because of a promise…," said Mr. Laurence. He ran his hands through his hair. "I suppose I'll forgive him. But he's a stubborn one!"

"So am I," said Jo. "But a kind word always works for me when nothing else will."

Mr. Laurence looked at this bold young woman. "And what do you suggest I do?" he asked.

"Why not send him a letter of apology," replied Jo. "I happen to know that Laurie loves letters. If you wrote him man to man, I'm sure all would be right again."

Mr. Laurence pinched Jo's cheek. His eyes were merry. "You're a sly one," he said. "But I don't mind being managed by you and Beth. I will write the letter this very minute!"

So Mr. Laurence wrote a letter of apology. And Jo slipped it under Laurie's door. Soon the matter was forgotten.

Only Meg remembered. She never spoke of Mr. Brooke. But she thought of him a great deal. And she dreamed dreams more than ever.

Chapter Twelve

Pleasant Meadows

The weeks that followed were as peaceful as sunshine after a storm. Beth improved daily. And Mr. March wrote that he hoped to return early in the new year.

On Christmas day a carpet of new snow covered the yard. Jo and Laurie had worked like elves at night making a Christmas surprise for Beth.

A snow princess stood in the yard. She carried a basket filled with fruit and flowers in one hand and a great roll of music in the other. Beth laughed when she saw it. Everyone was filled to the brim with happiness.

"I'm so full of happiness," said Beth. "I'm sure I couldn't hold another drop."

But the drop came!

"Here's another Christmas surprise for the March family!" announced Laurie, opening the door.

In walked Mr. March, leaning on Mr. Brooke's arm.

How the full hearts overflowed! Jo nearly fainted. Amy fell over a chair. And Mr. Brooke kissed Meg by mistake.

Excitement put strength into Beth's weak legs. She ran straight into her father's arms.

There never was such a Christmas dinner! Beth and Mr. March sat in one big armchair at the head of the table. Laurie and Mr. Laurence were there too. And so was Mr. Brooke.

Jo shot ugly looks at Mr. Brooke. He was still the enemy who might steal her Meg.

"I have noticed wonderful changes in my girls," said Mr. March. "They have, indeed, become little women."

"Oh, tell us what changes you see!" begged Meg.

"Here is one," said Father. He picked up Meg's hand. "I remember a time when this hand was white and smooth from lack of work. Your first care was to keep it that way. It's a much prettier hand now. I'm sure the sewing done by these pricked fingers will last a long time. You have learned that it is more important to work for a happy home than to have white hands. I am proud of you, Meg."

"And what about Jo?" asked Beth. "Please say something nice. She has been so very, very good to me."

"My tomboy Jo is gone," said Father. "In her place I see a young lady. She dresses neatly. She doesn't whistle, talk in slang, or lie on the rug anymore. I'll miss my wild girl. But this strong, helpful, tenderhearted woman delights me."

Jo's face grew rosy in the firelight. This praise from her father meant the world to her.

"Now Beth," said Amy, longing for her own turn.

"There's so little of her," said Father. "I don't want to say much. I'm afraid she will slip away. I see that she is not as shy as she used to be."

Father couldn't say another word. He was thinking how very nearly he had lost his dear daughter. He held Beth close. "I've got you safe, my Beth," he said tenderly. "And I'll keep you so, please God."

Turning to Amy, Father said, "I see that Amy waited her turn to be served at dinner. She helped her mother all afternoon. I see that she does not look in the mirror as much as she used to. I am proud to have a daughter with a talent for making life beautiful for herself and others."

It had been a hard year. The pilgrims had traveled a rough road. But now Father was back, and the way would be easier.

The March family had come at last to a pleasant meadow.

Chapter Thirteen

Meg and Mr. Brooke

It was the day after Christmas. Father rested in a big chair next to Beth's sofa. The rest of the family made sure they had everything they needed.

But Jo's happiness was clouded over by the thought of Mr. Brooke. She wasn't happy that he had stayed for dinner yesterday. She was even more unhappy that he had left his umbrella behind. Jo shook her fist at it. It meant he would be back.

Meg was silent. She was lost in thought. She blushed when anyone said Mr. Brooke's name. She jumped whenever the doorbell rang.

"She's probably waiting for *him*," thought Jo. Her mood grew darker.

Just then the doorbell rang, and Mr. Brooke walked in. Meg began to sew as though her life depended on it.

Jo went to get his umbrella. Mr. Brooke took that moment to tell Meg how he felt about her. He hoped she felt the same way.

"I'm too young," said Meg. Her cheeks were suddenly rosy.

"Please choose to love me, Meg," said Mr. Brooke. He spoke softly.

Meg looked at him. His brown eyes were both merry and tender. Meg remembered Annie Moffat's advice: "It doesn't suit women to be too willing."

"I *don't* choose to," said Meg, with a toss of her head. "Please go away and let me be!"

Poor Mr. Brooke looked as if his lovely castle in the air were falling around his ears. He had never seen Meg in such a mood before.

"Do you really mean that?" he asked.

"Yes, I do," said Meg. "I don't want to be worried about such things. Father says it's too soon."

"I'll wait," said Mr. Brooke. "I'll give you time to think about it."

"I wish you wouldn't," said Meg. She enjoyed testing her new power.

At that moment, who should enter the room but Aunt March. She had come to visit her nephew, Mr. March.

"Bless me, what's all this?" said Aunt March with a rap of her cane. "I suppose it's this young man who's making you look like a peony. You're not going to marry him, are you, child?" she asked.

Mr. Brooke had left the room.

"It's foolish to marry a poor man," warned Aunt March. "If you do, not one penny of my money will ever go to you."

Aunt March had a way of helping people make up their minds. If she had begged Meg to accept John Brooke, Meg would have refused. But the old woman's order made Meg angry.

"I shall marry whom I please, Aunt March," said Meg. "And you can leave your money to anyone you like."

"Highty tighty!" exclaimed Aunt March. "Is that the way you take my advice, miss? You'll be sorry for it. Living on love won't take you far. Don't spoil your whole life by making a mistake at the beginning."

"Father and Mother don't think it's a mistake," said Meg. "They like John. And so do I."

"Well, I wash my hands of the whole affair," said Aunt March. "Don't expect anything from me when you get married!"

Aunt March slammed the door in Meg's face and stormed off. She didn't

have the heart to visit Mr. March anymore.

Meg didn't know whether to laugh or
cry. Before she could make up her mind,
Mr. Brooke was back. He had heard every
word.

"I see you do care for me," he said.

"Yes, John," said Meg.

Jo came into the room, hoping her sister had sent the enemy away. She was
surprised to see the enemy and her sister
in an embrace.

"Sister Jo," said Mr. Brooke when he
saw her. "Congratulate us!"

This was too much. To lose her sister
to the enemy. But to be happy about it,
on top of that! Jo threw up her hands and
rushed out of the room.

She ran upstairs to break the news to
the rest of the family.

"Somebody go down quickly!" cried Jo.
"John Brooke is acting dreadfully. And
Meg likes it!"

Mr. and Mrs. March went downstairs. Jo threw herself onto her bed and wept bitterly. No one felt the way she did about Meg and John.

Beth and Amy were impressed with him. And Mr. and Mrs. March were happy to have him in the family. Even Laurie and Mr. Laurence joined in the celebration. They arrived with a big bouquet of flowers.

"You can't say nothing pleasant ever happens now, can you, Meg?" said Amy. She was preparing to sketch the happy couple.

"No, I'm sure I can't," replied Meg. And she smiled at John.

"I don't like this match," whispered Jo to Laurie. "I've lost my dearest friend. But I've made up my mind to bear it."

"You've still got me," replied Laurie. "When I'm done at college, you and I will go on trips together. I'll stand by you, Jo. All the days of my life!"

Jo smiled at Laurie. He had become such a good friend in just one year.

Father and Mother were sitting quietly in one corner. Amy was drawing Meg and Mr. Brooke. Beth lay on the sofa talking cheerily to Mr. Laurence.

Jo sat in her favorite seat with Laurie leaning on the back of her chair. She looked at the happy scene.

"I don't believe things could ever be better than this," said Jo.

Louisa May Alcott was born in Pennsylvania in 1832 and grew up in New England. She is best known for writing *Little Women*. The story is based on Alcott's own life. Like the March family, her family was very poor. She worked as a seamstress, a servant, and a teacher to help out.

Like Jo March, Alcott believed in equal rights for women. She was active in the movement to give women the right to vote.

Alcott wrote several other novels for children: *Little Men*, *Jo's Boys*, *An Old-Fashioned Girl*, and *Eight Cousins*. Louisa May Alcott died in 1888.

Monica Kulling was born in British Columbia, Canada. She has published two picture books, and many of her poems have appeared in *Cricket* magazine. Just like Jo March, Kulling prefers climbing trees to going to parties. She lives in Toronto, Canada, with her friend and their two dogs, Sophie and Alice.